Noddy

Collins *Children's Books*

It was a sunny day in Toy Town and
Noddy, Tessie Bear and Bumpy Dog
were enjoying a summer picnic
in the countryside.

They had brought googleberry muffins,
jam sandwiches and fresh lemonade.

"Delicious!" giggled Noddy,
as he ate his third muffin.

Suddenly, Noddy remembered a promise
he had made to Miss Pink Cat. He had
offered to meet her in Toy Town to help
set up the annual Ice Cream Festival.
But he had forgotten all about it!

"Poor Miss Pink Cat!" cried Noddy,
as he looked at his watch.

"Don't worry," Tessie Bear replied.
"We'll get back in time."

But secretly, Tessie Bear was very worried.

As they set off back to Toy
Town, they noticed a huge tree
that had fallen in the road ahead.

"The road is blocked!"
cried Tessie Bear.
"What shall we do, Noddy?"

Noddy thought for a while.
He knew that the tree was too heavy
to lift. They couldn't go over it.
They couldn't go under it.
There was only one option left.

"Let's go back!" cried Noddy.
"I know a secret path that will take
us straight to Toy Town."

"Well done, Noddy," smiled Tessie Bear.
"Maybe we'll make it after all!"

So the friends whizzed back
the way they came, to find
Noddy's secret path.

Noddy was so happy that he'd
remembered the secret path that
he forgot to look where he was going.

As he turned round to tell Bumpy Dog
a joke, Tessie Bear squealed.

"Noddy! Watch out!" she cried.

"splash!"

Noddy had driven straight into a big pond!

"Oh dear!" said Noddy, as he peered
at the water underneath his taxi.

"Now what are we going to do?"
cried Tessie Bear. "Poor Miss Pink Cat
won't be able to set up alone!"

The ducks in the pond started
quacking as Noddy, Tessie Bear
and Bumpy Dog leaped
out of the car.

Then Noddy had an idea.
If he could find Mr Jumbo, he could
slurp up the water with his trunk!

"But how will you find him?" asked Tessie
Bear, when she heard Noddy's plan.

Noddy knew that Mr Jumbo went for a
walk on the main road every afternoon,
so ran off to find him.

Finding the road wasn't as easy as Noddy had thought. The secret path was full of obstacles.

Poor Noddy had to run through fields, over streams and climb over a high fence to reach the main road.

By the time he reached the road he was dreaming of cold googleberry ice cream.

Noddy looked at his watch. It was half past one.

"Only half an hour before the Ice Cream Festival begins!" thought Noddy.

Suddenly, Noddy spotted Mr Jumbo strolling along the road.

"Mr Jumbo! We need your help!" Noddy cried, as he explained about his taxi floating on the pond.

"Cold water? I'm so very thirsty!" Mr Jumbo laughed. "Let's go!"

By the time Noddy and Mr Jumbo got back
to the pond, the taxi was sinking fast.
But with a few giant slurps from Mr Jumbo's
trunk, the pond was soon dry.

"Thanks, Mr Jumbo!" said Noddy happily,
as he jumped back in to his taxi.

"Great idea, Noddy!"
laughed Tessie Bear, as they
set off towards Toy Town.
"Whatever would we do
without your good ideas?"

"Let's just hope we don't bump into any more problems along the way," Noddy said, as they set off further down the secret path.

Just then, Noddy looked around. The trees looked different. The flowers looked different. Even the colour of the grass looked different. And there was a big brick wall at the end of the road.

"Uh oh," said Noddy. "Tessie Bear, Bumpy Dog, I think we are lost!"

"We don't even have a map!"
Tessie Bear said,
as she got out of the car.

Noddy sat on the grass and tried
to think of what to do next.
Suddenly, he had an idea.

"Bumpy Dog!" exclaimed Noddy.
"Can you sniff your way
back to Toy Town?"

Bumpy Dog nodded his head and
started running off down the path.
He began barking and pointing
at something by a tree.

"A sign," said Noddy.
"Pointing to Toy Town!"
laughed Tessie Bear.
"We might just make it after all!"
said Noddy, happily.
"Well done, Bumpy Dog!"

Finally, Toy Town was in sight. With ten minutes to go before the big event, the friends had made it!

"At last!" cried Miss Pink Cat, when she saw Noddy running over to the Ice Cream Parlour. "Sorry, Miss Pink Cat!" said Noddy, out of breath. "You could say I have had a rather unusual day!"

Noddy made up for lost time by covering Toy Town in colourful ice cream decorations.

"Thank you for your help today."
said Noddy to Tessie Bear,
when everything was ready.
"And Bumpy Dog and Mr Jumbo!
Without you, we would never have
got back to Toy Town in time
to help Miss Pink Cat."

The Toy Town friends
grabbed some spoons
and filled themselves with
the sweetest ice-cream
they had ever tasted.

First published in the UK by HarperCollins Children's Books in 2008

1 3 5 7 9 10 8 6 4 2
ISBN-13: 978-0-00-725897-0
ISBN-10: 0-00-725897-6

Printed and bound in China

NODDY™